This igloo book belongs to:

....

igloobooks

Published in 2017
by Igloo Books Ltd
Cottage Farm
Sywell
NN6 0BJ
www.igloobooks.com

Written by Caroline Richards
Illustrated by Louise Anglicas

Designed by Hannah George
Edited by Hannah Campling and Hannah Cather

REX001 1017
2 4 6 8 10 9 7 5 3 1
ISBN 978-1-78670-476-4

Printed and manufactured in China

The
Power
of Love

igloobooks

Little Bear had been playing

in the bright and sunny wood.

But soon the trees cast long shadows

on the path where he stood.

It was nearly time for supper
and very soon it would be night.
Little Bear wasn't sure if home
was down the left path or the right.

Just then, some woodland friends appeared, as the sun was sinking low.

"If you need help to find your way," one squeaked, "the fireflies will know."

"They have special powers that will safely light your way.

But you must believe in magic, or their light will go away!"

Up sprang a magical firefly,

to Little Bear's surprise.

"Think of a happy memory," he buzzed,

"then wish and close your eyes."

He shut his eyes and thought of when Mummy took him to the sea.

They paddled, then made sandcastles and ate ice cream for their tea.

"When you remember things you love, it makes us shine and glow." As Firefly explained, all their bright lights started to grow.

Little Bear missed his cosy cave.

He longed to be snuggled in bed.

So he shut his eyes tight.

"My memories are magic!" he said.

Then, Little Bear remembered something that made his heart feel warm.

Once, he and Daddy baked some cookies when there had been a storm.

"We'll guide you home," said Firefly.

"With each memory you recall,

we'll glow brighter with the power of love

and then you won't be scared at all."

Sure enough, more fireflies came,

as Little Bear walked through the wood.

They shone brighter as he thought

of the nicest memories he could.

Little Bear felt big and brave,

walking beside his magical friends.

They travelled across a bridge, over

a stream full of twists and bends.

Then suddenly, he saw a shape, and something big flew overhead.

A beak, huge wings and two beady eyes. "Who's there?" Little Bear said.

He forgot all his happy memories, so the fireflies lost their spark.

Because he was afraid of the scary shape, the wood turned cold and dark.

TWIT-TWOO! "I'm just a friendly owl," said a voice from a branch above.

"Remember, if you want to get home, you must use the power of love."

With all of his might, Little Bear thought of his sweetest memory of home.

Cuddled close with Mummy and Daddy, with them he was never alone.

With a WHOOSH of magic, the
fireflies all burst back into light.
They lit the path to take Little Bear
home to cuddles, warm and tight.

There at the door stood
Mummy and Daddy, their
arms thrown open wide.
They snuggled him close
and kissed his nose,
then carried him inside.

"I've been on an adventure!" Little Bear cried, "and made new friends, too. They taught me about the power of love and helped me get back to you."

Little Bear had found his way home with the love inside his heart.

He was back with Mummy and Daddy, and they'd never be apart.